Jim

story and pictures by

Ruth Bornstein

A CLARION BOOK
THE SEABURY PRESS • NEW YORK

for Adam

The Seabury Press,
815 Second Avenue, New York, New York 10017

Library of Congress Cataloging in Publication Data

Bornstein, Ruth.   Jim.
"A Clarion book."
Summary: When Jim the dog searches for his father who has not re-
turned from a day of exploring, he discovers more than he expects.
[1. Dogs—Fiction]   I. Title.
PZ7.B64848Ji   [E]   77-12712   ISBN 0-8164-3204-X

There was a young dog and his name was Jim.
And he was all alone in the world.

505

It hadn't always been that way. Until last spring Jim lived
together with his father, an old dog. Then, one morning
Jim's father lifted his nose and sniffed. "Jim, my son," he said,
"there is a delicious smell on the wind. I'll be back before dark."

And Jim's father had followed his nose across the field, into the woods . . .
and had never come back.

Now summer was here. Jim lay awake in the night and thought about his father.

He remembered how his father loved to sniff and snuff under every bush. He remembered how his father loved to sing in the night when the moon was full.

Jim lifted his nose and looked up at the sky. Tonight there was no moon. The sky was dark. He sniffed. There was only a lonely smell in the air. "Oh, where is my father now?" said Jim.

With the first light of day, Jim got up,
gave himself a good stretch and a scratch and said,
"I'm not going to stay here. I'm going out into the world to find my father."

The trail was old, the scent was faint. Before him the woods
stood silent and unknown. Jim gave himself a good shake.
With hope in his heart and his nose to the ground,
he went out into the world following his father's trail.

Hard on the trail he came to the woods.
Suddenly Jim stopped. He sniffed.
Something was coming up the trail!

But it was not his father.
Jim went on, following his father's trail.

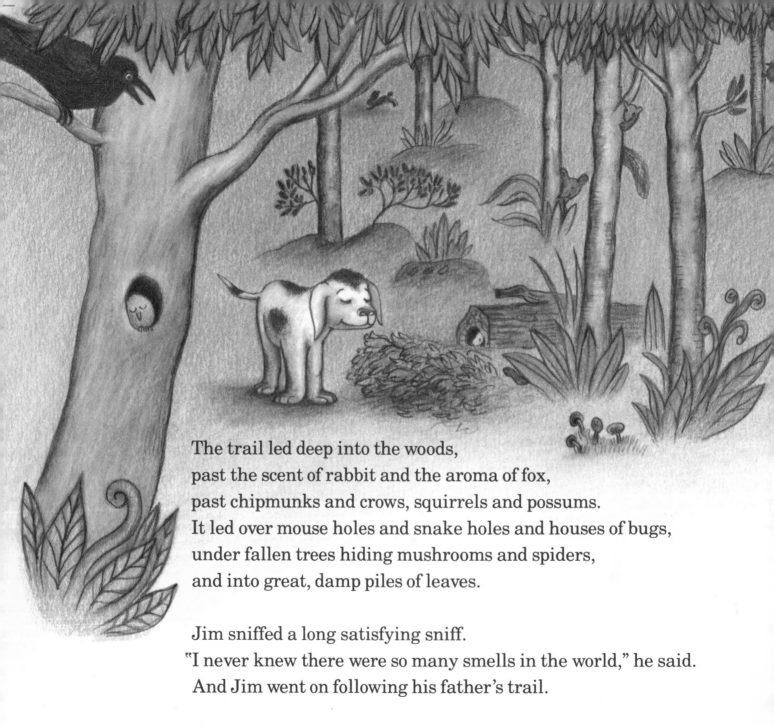

The trail led deep into the woods,
  past the scent of rabbit and the aroma of fox,
  past chipmunks and crows, squirrels and possums.
  It led over mouse holes and snake holes and houses of bugs,
  under fallen trees hiding mushrooms and spiders,
  and into great, damp piles of leaves.

  Jim sniffed a long satisfying sniff.
"I never knew there were so many smells in the world," he said.
  And Jim went on following his father's trail.

Then, fast on the trail, he came to a cave.
"I wonder who lives here," said Jim.

All at once another scent crossed the trail.

Huckleberries!

Jim tasted a huckleberry. Then another. Then another.
Jim's mouth was full of huckleberries. He didn't notice a new scent
coming closer and closer.

Just in time Jim lifted his nose out of the huckleberry patch.
With a yelp, he dove into the bushes . . .

. . . tore through the brambles, fell into a marsh, splashed toward the river,

grabbed hold of an old log, kicked hard with his paws . . .

. . . and he was safe!
But he was in the middle of a wide river,
and his father's trail was lost.

"How will I ever find my father now?" said Jim.

The river rushed by, cold and dark.
Jim sniffed at the water.
The river gave out a marvelous smell of fish.
He sniffed at the air. It smelled fresh and crisp.
Jim's nose even caught the scent of pine trees
on an island in the river.

Jim breathed deep. "Well, at least I'm alive,
a young dog out in the world,
and there are good smells all around me."

But Jim saw that the sun was low. Soon night would fall.
Flat on the log, Jim paddled hard for the island.

The current tried to pull him the other way. Jim paddled fast and furiously.
With his last ounce of strength, he hauled the log up on the island.
In the dim light he saw a boat smashed on the rocks.

Just then the moon rose slowly over the river.
The moon was huge and full, round and yellow.
A moon just like the one his father had sung to long ago.

Jim felt something slow and sweet stir inside his chest.
A lump rose to his throat. Jim couldn't help it. He threw back his head,
opened his mouth and was about to howl.

Then his nose caught a scent.

Jim's tail popped up. His ears popped up.
He sniffed. He sniffed all over the ground.

He stopped. Through the trees he could hear a voice.
A voice singing sad and low.

"Oh, here I am, shipwrecked and alone.
Long ago I went out to roam.
My little son must be almost grown.
Oh, here I am, and here I moan."

Jim's nose trembled. His jaw trembled. His tail began to thump slowly,
then faster and faster.

With a mighty leap, he burst through the trees.

"Father!"
"Son!"
   And there on an island in the middle of a river
   there was a wiggling and a waggling, a prancing and a dancing,
   and many laughing barks.

When they calmed down at last,
Jim's father told him how he had been chased by a bear,
how he had escaped just in time in a boat he found by the river,
how he had been wrecked on the island by a stormy current. . . .
Suddenly Jim barked. "Wait Father!"

Jim's nose pointed up in the air. He sniffed. He sniffed again.
A cool wind carried the scent of places far down the river.
"Father," barked Jim, "it's time we were on our way.
The smells are delicious!"
The old dog's nose quivered. "But how can we go?"

Proudly Jim led his father to the log he'd left at the edge of the island.
The old dog's eyes lit up. "Jim, my son, you have saved us."
Jim helped his father onto the log, gave a push, and jumped on behind.

As the two dogs sailed out into the world toward new adventures,
they lifted their noses to the night,

and with their voices blending in perfect harmony,

they made beautiful music together.